Carlos & Carmen

The Big Rain

by Kirsten McDonald
illustrated by Erika Meza

Calico Kid

An Imprint of Magic Wagon
abdopublishing.com

For Anita – Gracias por las palabras en español —KKM

To my two Carlos, and specially both of my parents; who taught me to value changes, movings, carnes asadas, mischiefs, surprises and the beautiful moments you can only live with your family. Gracias: ilos quiero! —EM

abdopublishing.com

Printed in the United States of America, North Mankato, Minnesota.
102015
012016

THIS BOOK CONTAINS
RECYCLED MATERIALS

Written by Kirsten McDonald
Illustrated by Erika Meza
Edited by Heidi M.D. Elston
Designed by Candice Keimig

Library of Congress Cataloging-in-Publication Data

McDonald, Kirsten, author.
  The big rain / by Kirsten McDonald ; illustrated by Erika Meza.
    pages cm. -- (Carlos & Carmen)
  Summary: After a three-day rainstorm, twins Carlos and Carmen go out to play in their wet and muddy backyard--and soon their parents join in the fun.
  ISBN 978-1-62402-137-4
  1. Hispanic American families--Juvenile fiction. 2. Twins--Juvenile fiction. 3. Brothers and sisters--Juvenile fiction. 4. Rain and rainfall--Juvenile fiction. 5. Play--Juvenile fiction. [1. Twins--Fiction. 2. Brothers and sisters--Fiction. 3. Family life--Fiction. 4. Rain and rainfall--Fiction. 5. Play--Fiction. 6. Hispanic Americans--Fiction.] I. Meza, Erika, illustrator. II. Title.
  PZ7.1.M4344Bi 2016
  [E]--dc23
                                    2015026225

Table of Contents

Chapter 1
Rainy Days

On Monday, it started to rain. It rained all day and all night. On Tuesday, it rained again. On Wednesday, there was even more rain.

"I'm tired of all this rain," complained Carlos.

"Yo también," Carmen agreed. "I want to play on the tire swing."

"I just want to go outside," said Carlos. He flopped down on his twin's bed. Spooky, their cat, jumped up beside Carlos.

"There's nada to do," Carlos added as he rubbed Spooky's soft, black fur.

"Yeah," Carmen agreed, "nothing except watch it rain."

Outside, the puddles got bigger. Outside, the puddles got deeper. Outside, it kept raining and raining and raining.

Chapter 2
No More Rain

On Thursday, Carlos woke up early. He could not hear any rain falling. He ran to Carmen's room and bounced on her bed.

"Wake up, Carmen! Wake up!" he said. "It stopped raining."

"Really?" said Carmen as she jumped out of bed.

The twins raced to the window. They looked out at their backyard.

They saw the tree with the tire
swing. They saw the fence that
marked the edge of their yard.

But mostly, they saw water. Lots
and lots of water. Their big backyard
had become the biggest puddle they
had ever seen.

"There's a lot of water down there,"
said Carlos.

"There's enough agua to be a lake,"
said Carmen.

Carlos looked at Carmen. Carmen looked at Carlos. And, they both began to smile.

"Are you thinking what I'm thinking?" they asked at the same time. And, because they were twins, they were.

Chapter 3
The Biggest Puddle

Carlos and Carmen got dressed in a flash. They raced downstairs to the kitchen where Mamá and Papá were drinking coffee.

"What's the big rush, mis amores?" asked Mamá.

"It stopped raining!" said Carlos.

"And, we're going outside to play," added Carmen.

"But everything's wet outside," said Mamá.

"We know," said Carlos with a smile.

"And everything's muddy," said Papá.

"We know," said Carmen with an
even bigger smile.

The twins rushed out to the deck.

Carlos said, "Watch my big splash!"
He jumped off the deck.

"That's nothing," said Carmen.
"¡Mira!" She took a running start and
leaped off the deck.

When Carmen landed, water splashed into the air. Water splashed onto the deck. Water splashed all over Carlos.

Carlos looked down at his wet shirt and his wet shorts. He looked at Carmen in her dry shirt and her dry shorts.

"Two can play this game," Carlos laughed. He gave the water a sweeping kick.

The water splashed up into the air. Then the water splashed down all over Carmen.

Carmen looked down at her wet shirt and her wet shorts. She laughed, "I'm going to get you!"

"Only if you can catch me!" Carlos shouted as he ran splashing through the water.

Chapter 4
Muddy Mess

Carlos and Carmen sloshed from
the backyard puddle to the deck.
They were very wet and very happy.
They were also very muddy.

"We can't go inside like this," said Carlos. "Mamá will go loca if we bring all this mud and agua into the house."

Together they called, "Mamá! Mamá!"

Mamá opened the back door. She looked at her two wet, muddy children.

"¡Dios mío!" Mamá exclaimed.
"What happened to you two?"

"Umm . . . we got wet?" said
Carlos.

"And muddy?" Carmen added.

"Tell me something I don't already
know," said Mamá, shaking her head.

"¿Qué pasa?" asked Papá as he
came to the door.

Mamá and Papá looked at the backyard puddle. They looked at their two wet, muddy children. Then Mamá and Papá looked at each other.

Papá smiled at Mamá, but Carlos and Carmen did not see it. Mamá winked at Papá, but the twins did not see that either.

"Hijos, wait right there," said Mamá as she and Papá hurried out of the kitchen.

"I think we're in trouble," said Carlos.

"Yeah," agreed Carmen. "Wet, muddy trouble."

Carlos and Carmen sat down on the deck. Carlos worried about the water. Carmen worried about the mud.

Chapter 5
¡Mira!

At last, Carlos and Carmen heard
Mamá and Papá walking through the
kitchen. The twins looked at each
other.

They were very surprised when Papá walked onto the deck in his bathing suit. He was carrying a big blue lump.

They were even more surprised when Mamá came out. She was wearing her bathing suit. And, she was carrying a red pump.

The twins watched as Papá unrolled his bundle, and Mamá pumped it up. They watched as Papá

pushed the air mattress onto the
steps, and Mamá turned on the hose.

Carlos looked at Carmen and said,
"I think, maybe, we're not in trouble."

"¡Mira!" shouted Papá, and he
slid down the air mattress into the
backyard puddle.

"¡Mira!" shouted Mamá as
she slid down.

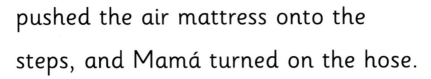

Carmen jumped up. "We're not in trouble. We're in fun! Come on!"

For the rest of the morning, everyone slid down the homemade water slide. They chased each other in their backyard puddle. They laughed, and they ran, and they splashed.

As they ate lunch, Carlos said, "Three days of rain was really boring.

But this morning I had a week's worth of fun."

"Yeah," said Carmen. Then she added with a big smile, "After lunch, let's go see if we can make it two weeks' worth of fun."

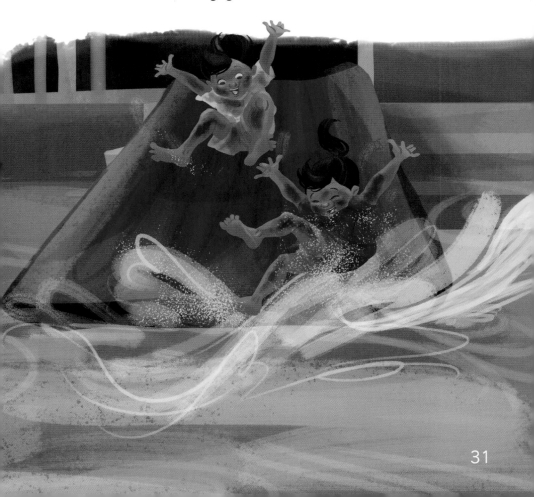

Spanish to English

agua – water

¡Dios mío! – Goodness gracious!

hijos – children

loca – crazy

Mamá – Mommy

¡Mira! – Look!

mis amores – my loves

nada – nothing

Papá – Daddy

¿Qué pasa? – What's up?

yo también – me too